DREAMWORKS
SHE-RA
PRINCESSE

D0832315

SONG of the SEA WITCH

BY TRACEY WEST

ILLUSTRATED BY HEDVIG
HÄGGMAN-SUND

SCHOLASTIC INC.

Copyright © 2019 DreamWorks Animation LLC. All Rights Reserved. SHE-RA and associated trademarks and character copyrights are owned by and used under license from Mattel, Inc. Portions of text based on screenplays by Noelle Stevenson.

ISBN 978-1-338-58103-4

10 9 8 7 6 5 4 3 2 1   19 20 21 22 23

Printed in the U.S.A.   40

First printing 2019

CONTENTS

The World of Etheria 1

Chapter 1: A Mysterious Message 7

Chapter 2: A Surprise in Salineas 21

Chapter 3: Catra's Plan 33

Chapter 4: Captured! 41

Chapter 5: The Story of the Sea Sorceress 53

Chapter 6: Monster Trouble 65

Chapter 7: The Sound of Victory 73

Chapter 8: What Did We Forget . . . ? 81

Chapter 9: Hey, Adora! 85

Chapter 10: Trust 95

THE WORLD OF
ETHERIA

On a planet called Etheria, two forces battle for control.

The Horde, with its skillfully trained soldiers and advanced technology, has one goal: to conquer all of Etheria in the name of Hordak.

The other force, the Rebellion, is made up of princesses from across the planet. A series of heartbreaking defeats left the alliance broken for years—until one fateful day, a hero rose among them and reunited them once more.

Adora, a Horde soldier, discovered the sword that transforms her into She-Ra, the hero whose destiny was written by the First Ones a thousand years ago. With She-Ra leading the princesses, the alliance delivered a crushing defeat to the Horde at the battle of Bright Moon.

But Lord Hordak, the leader of the Horde, has no plans to give up. With the help of a fallen princess, he is creating newer, better weapons and technology. He will not stop until the princesses are defeated once and for all.

As their story unfolds, meet Adora and some of the characters who will determine the fate of Etheria . . .

ADORA

Raised by the Horde, Adora believed she was doing good. But when she finds a mythical sword that unlocks her power as She-Ra, Adora is driven to fight for Etheria as a leader of the Rebellion.

ABILITIES: Adora is a clever problem solver, a fast and athletic soldier, and a brave fighter.

SHE-RA

When Adora raises the sword and pledges to fight "for the honor of Grayskull," she is transformed into the mythical warrior princess She-Ra. Adora retains her personality and sense of self, but she's taller and stronger—and has much better hair.

POWERS: Super-strength, shapeshifting sword, limited healing powers, connection to the ancient First Ones of Etheria

THE HORDE

CATRA

Catra and Adora were both orphans and were best friends growing up in the Horde. Catra is a prankster with a villainous streak that she is forced to explore once Adora discovers the sword.

ABILITIES: She's cunning and fast, with catlike reflexes.

SCORPIA

Even though she is a force captain in the Horde, Scorpia has a good heart. But she's eager to please her superiors, especially Catra, and that makes her a fierce opponent.

POWERS: She has a poisonous scorpion tail and above-average strength.

HORDAK

The evil leader of the Horde is bent on world domination. The Horde recruits rarely see him, as he prefers to plot from the depths of his lab.

ABILITY: He has a brilliant technological mind.

THE REBELLION

GLIMMER

The princess of Bright Moon is driven to find her own path and is an enthusiastic leader of the Rebellion. She has inherited magical powers from her mother, but her magic is limited, which can make her feel insecure at times.

POWERS: Teleportation, energy blasts, sparkle powers

BOW

Glimmer's best friend is a good guy who values loyalty and honor above everything else. He will do anything for his friends— and even complete strangers.

ABILITIES: He's an expert archer and a whiz with technology.

QUEEN ANGELLA

She is Glimmer's mother and the immortal queen of Bright Moon. After the tragic death of her husband at the hands of the Horde, she is overprotective of her daughter.

POWER: Flight

MERMISTA

The princess of Salineas is brutally honest, but she sometimes keeps her real feelings hidden so that no one will see her soft side. She is a powerful ally to the Rebellion. **POWERS:** She can control water and transform her legs into a mermaid's tail.

SEA HAWK

This pirate loves to sing sea shanties and tell stories bragging of his ocean adventures. He began as a friend to Mermista, but soon became a valuable member of the team to save Etheria. **ABILITY:** His confidence is his greatest asset.

CHAPTER 1
A MYSTERIOUS MESSAGE

"The Rebellion is unstoppable!" Glimmer was saying. "Taking that fortress from the Horde was an impressive exercise in teamwork!"

In a shower of purple sparkles, she teleported from her nest-like bed near the ceiling of her bedroom and materialized next to Adora. Her mouth in a determined line, Adora practiced fencing moves with her sword while Glimmer talked.

"Perfuma created that giant Plant Golem that swatted away the Horde soldiers on foot," Glimmer went on. "Frosta pummeled those Horde bots with her ice fists! Mermista combined her waves with Bow's electric arrows to fry the Horde's laser cannons. It was amazing!"

"Definitely," Adora agreed, thrusting at an invisible enemy.

"And after Bow stopped that Kyle kid with one of his net arrows, I saved Bow from being blasted by that lizard guy," Glimmer said.

Bow was sitting cross-legged on the floor at a low table in a corner of the room.

"Yeah, thanks for that," Bow said, keeping his eyes on the tiny wooden figure he was painting.

Glimmer turned back to Adora. "And Adora, you—"

"—let Scorpia knock my sword out of my hands after I transformed into She-Ra," Adora replied. "If you hadn't distracted her, I might be—"

"But that's exactly what teamwork is all about!" Glimmer pointed out. "When one of us is in trouble, another one of us is right there to back them up."

Adora nodded. "I know. But a team is only as strong as its weakest member. And I've got to work on my sword skills." She spun in a circle, holding her sword out in front of her.

Bow looked up. "You're not saying you're a weak link, are you?" he asked. "Because you're the only one of us who can transform into an eight-foot-tall superstrong warrior with amazing powers."

"Powers that are no good without the skill to back them up," Adora said.

Her life before she had become She-Ra seemed like an eternity ago, but it was really only a few months. It all began when she discovered the sword in the Whispering Woods. The sword was linked to her, somehow, and when she held it over her head and said, "For the honor of Grayskull!" she transformed into She-Ra, Princess of Power.

She'd had to quickly decide whether she wanted to stay with the Horde, the fighting force from the Fright Zone dedicated to defeating the princesses of Etheria—or use her new powers to join the princesses and stop the Horde.

She chose the princesses, turning her back on her best friend, Catra, a force captain in the Horde. That began a chain reaction that resulted in a huge fight, the battle of Bright Moon. The princesses won that battle, but Catra wasn't giving up. Every day there was a new battle to fight.

I have to be stronger, better, faster, Adora told

herself. *We have to defeat the Horde and save Etheria once and for all!*

Glimmer touched the end of Adora's sword and gently lowered it.

"You're being too hard on yourself, Adora," she said. "The Rebellion is going to win this fight. After our last battle, I'm more confident than ever. I can't wait for our next strategy session."

"I wish the other princesses hadn't gone back to their kingdoms," Bow said. "I just can't seem to get the details right on their battle figures."

"Let me see," Glimmer said, and she teleported over to him.

Bow had created what he called a "war table" so that they could plot out battle strategies using pieces that represented the members of the Rebellion and their opponents. He'd started out by carving and painting figures of himself, Glimmer, and She-Ra, but now the other princesses wanted their own.

The original figures stood in the center of the board: She-Ra with her flowing mane of golden hair, Glimmer with her pink-and-purple hair and blue cape, and Bow grasping a tiny bow and arrow.

Circling them were the other finished figures. Perfuma, with her long, pale hair and pink-and-green gown. Frosta, shorter than all the rest, with her fur-trimmed jacket and blue hair. Spinnerella's purple leotard and tights matched her long, purple hair, and Netossa's figure had a sweep of white hair over one side of her face.

In his hand, Bow held a battle figure wearing a gold-and-turquoise outfit.

"I can't get the shade of Mermista's hair just right," Bow complained.

"It should be a little more blue, less green," Glimmer offered.

Bow nodded. "You're right!" He dipped his paint-brush into a little jar of blue paint.

"Actually, can you finish that later?" Glimmer asked him. "Mom is expecting us to give her a report on the battle at the fortress."

Bow stuck out his tongue as he concentrated on painting, adding blue strokes to Mermista's hair. "Almost got it . . . perfect!" he announced.

"Yeah, that's good," Glimmer agreed. "You've managed to capture that 'I don't care' look on her face just right."

Adora tucked her sword into her belt. "Mermista *does* care," she remarked. "She just doesn't want anyone to know that she does."

It had taken a little while for Adora to understand the princess from Salineas. Mermista was brutally honest and acted as if nothing or nobody impressed her. But she had quickly proven that she cared about a lot of things, including saving Etheria and protecting her friends. The Rebellion wouldn't be the same without her.

"Well, I'm sure she's going to have a problem with her battle figure," Bow said. "But I tried my best." He put the figure down on the war table.

"Are we ready?" Glimmer asked. "Mom's waiting."

"Sure, let's go," Adora said.

The three friends left Glimmer's room and walked through the gleaming marble halls of Bright Moon Castle. They passed a line of guards, majestic in their flowing robes and face masks. They headed down a staircase to the throne room of Queen Angella—Glimmer's mom.

The queen's large, pale pink wings shimmered— they mesmerized Adora every time she saw them.

Queen Angella's long hair, the same shades of pink and purple as Glimmer's, cascaded down her shoulders.

"Glimmer, Adora, Bow, it's good to see you," she said in her warm, friendly voice. "Now, tell me—what happened at the fortress?"

"It was awesome!" Glimmer began, but before she could say any more, a Bright Moon guard marched into the room.

"Announcing a messenger from the kingdom of Salineas!"

Adora and her friends turned. A man with long, blue hair wearing a turquoise uniform walked in. He bowed to Queen Angella.

"Queen Angella of Bright Moon, I bring a message from Queen Calypsa of Salineas."

"Queen Calypsa? Don't you mean Princess Mermista?" Glimmer asked.

The messenger shook his head. "Her Majesty Calypsa is the new queen of Salineas. She has not decided whether Salineas will continue to support the Rebellion or will give their allegiance to the Horde."

Queen Angella's eyes narrowed. "Who is this Calypsa, and what claim does she have on Salineas?"

"And what about Mermista? Is she okay?" Adora asked.

"All questions will be answered once you meet with Queen Calypsa in Salineas," the messenger replied.

Adora stepped in front of him and put her hand on her sword. "Sorry, but I need an answer now. Is Mermista all right?"

"She is alive, but . . ." The messenger nervously looked away. "I can say no more."

Adora took a step closer to him. "I think you can."

Queen Angella stood up. "Adora, please back down," she said. "We must not blame the messenger. I will go to Salineas and find out what is happening."

"No, Mom, let *us* go," Glimmer said. "Mermista is our friend. Something weird is happening in Salineas, and we have to help her!"

Her mother considered this. "I understand," she said. "You have a connection to Mermista. You, Adora, and Bow shall go."

"I was supposed to . . . Calypsa asked for the queen of Bright Moon," the messenger stammered.

Now it was Glimmer's turn to get in his face. "What? The princess of Bright Moon isn't good enough?"

"I—I'm sure that will be fine," the messenger said, and he hurried out of the throne room.

"There is no time to waste!" Adora said. "We've got to get to Salineas and save Mermista!"

CHAPTER 2
A SURPRISE IN SALINEAS

A riot of noise streamed out of the tavern in the coastal town of Seaworthy. Accordions played, pirates sang, and tough customers argued, joked, and laughed.

"Sea Hawk must be in here somewhere," Adora said as she entered with Glimmer and Bow. The sea captain was a friend of Mermista's—and a big help to the Rebellion.

"I'm sure he'll take us right to Mermista on his ship when he hears what we've got to say," Glimmer remarked.

"Does he still have a ship, or did he set fire to the last one?" Bow asked. "I've lost track."

"I'm sure he'll know how to get one," Adora replied.

They approached the tavern's server—a muscled woman with purple skin and a shock of short, white hair.

"Is Sea Hawk here?" Adora asked.

"Hasn't been around here for days," the server grunted in reply.

Bow gasped. "Days? Do you have any idea what happened to him?" he asked.

The woman shrugged and turned away from them.

"I have a bad feeling about this," Glimmer said, frowning. "First Mermista, and now Sea Hawk."

"Sea Hawk might just be on one of his adventures," Adora said. "But you could be right. Now it's even more important than ever that we get to

Salineas right away. We need to get to the bottom of this. We'll just have to find another boat."

"Did you say you needed a boat?"

Adora turned to see a woman wearing a crisp blue uniform a shade darker than her eyes.

"They call me Liana," she said. "I couldn't help but overhear—I can take you to Salineas."

"Awesome!" Adora said. "What's your price? Do you want me to arm wrestle you, and if I win, we get a free ride?"

"That's . . . not necessary. I'm going that way, anyway," Liana explained. "You're welcome to come with me."

"Thank you, Liana," Glimmer said, and they followed her out of the tavern.

"What kind of a name is Liana for a sea captain?" Bow whispered to Glimmer and Adora as they walked. "I thought all captains had names like Sea Hawk, or Shark Slayer, or Wave Rider!"

"I don't think it matters," Glimmer answered. "Besides, it seems like she knows what she's talking about."

Liana led them to a sturdy-looking ship. It wasn't big, but it would be large enough for all of them.

"Help me weigh the anchor and hoist the sails, and we'll be on our way," Liana said.

Adora, Glimmer, and Bow got to work with the no-nonsense captain. They grabbed the arms of the capstan, a rotating post on the deck that was attached to the anchor with chains. Once they raised the anchor, they helped her unleash the sails.

"Um, shouldn't you be singing sea shanties while we do this?" Bow asked.

"No," Liana replied.

"Oh. Well, Sea Hawk always sings sea shanties," Bow said. "So I thought . . ."

"Nope," Liana said. "Can't stand them. I'd rather listen to the wind and the birds."

Without another word, their captain set sail. There was a pleasant breeze and a calm ocean as they sailed to Salineas, but the three friends each churned with worry as they made their way to Mermista's island kingdom. What was going on there?

After a few hours, Salineas appeared on the horizon: a city of pale purple coral structures adorned with seashells rising from purple stone. Mermista's palace towered above them all, with spiraling turrets that kissed the bright blue sky.

Liana steered the boat into the harbor.

"Thanks, Liana," Bow said. "Are you going to go set your boat on fire now?"

Liana frowned. "Why would I do that?"

Bow sighed. "Never mind," he said. "I guess I just miss Sea Hawk. I hope he's okay."

"If he's in trouble, we'll figure it out," Adora said.

They said goodbye to Liana and walked onto the shore, where two Salinean guards waited for them. Adora marched up to them.

"You have to tell us what is going on!" she demanded. "Who is this Queen Calypsa? And what happened to Mermista?"

The two guards exchanged glances.

"We cannot say," one of them replied.

The other one looked around nervously. "In our hearts, we still serve the princess," he said. "But we must obey Queen Calypsa now."

"But why?" Glimmer asked.

"If we tell you, Mermista's life will be in danger," he

answered. "Now come, let us bring you to the queen."

For a split second, Adora thought about using force to make the guards tell her what was going on. She'd learned how to do that while training in the Horde. But she didn't want to hurt them, and if they were telling the truth, it was best to play along until she, Glimmer, and Bow saw for themselves what had happened to Mermista.

They walked toward the palace. The people of Salineas shuffled through the streets, their heads down. One little girl looked up at Adora as she passed, giving her a hopeful glance.

What is everyone so afraid of? Adora wondered.

As they got closer to the palace, Adora saw the Salineas Sea Gate rising behind it. Connected to Mermista's runestone, the Pearl, the gate was a magical barrier that protected Salineas—and the ocean passage to Bright Moon—from the Fright Zone, the land of the Horde.

Normally, the protection could be seen as a magical light between the two arches made of giant statues shaped like women. But now there was no light.

"What happened to the gate?" Adora asked.

"Queen Calypsa wants it open so that her guests from the Horde may be welcomed," the guard replied.

"You mean the Horde is on its way here?" Adora asked, alarmed. "When are they supposed to arrive?"

"Any day now," the guard answered. "Hordak received his invitation the same day that Queen Angella received hers."

Adora, Glimmer, and Bow looked at one another with wide eyes, and seemed to silently agree to remain calm.

"I don't understand why *anybody* would leave their doors open to the Horde," Glimmer said. "When I meet this Queen Calypsa, I'm gonna—"

They had reached the throne room doors. The guards swung them open.

"Queen Calypsa awaits," they said.

The three friends cautiously stepped into the throne room. Waterfalls cascaded down from the ceiling, next to murals covered with strange symbols—the language of the First Ones of Etheria.

"Come, representatives of Bright Moon!" Queen Calypsa demanded.

She sat on Mermista's throne, wearing a crown of pearls atop the green hair piled high on her head.

She had pale green skin, and fins sprouted from both sides of her neck. Her gown looked as if it was made of shimmering green fish scales.

Mermista stood next to her. She rolled her eyes when she saw Adora, Bow, and Glimmer.

"Wow, this is embarrassing," she said.

"Mermista! You're all right!" Glimmer cried.

"Well, not exactly," Mermista replied. "This fish lady came, and she kind of tricked me, and I should probably warn you—"

"Silence!" Queen Calypsa shrieked, and she pointed at Mermista. A green ring glittered on the queen's finger.

Mermista's own hand flew to her mouth, covering it. At the same time, Adora noticed a strange amulet around Mermista's neck. The green stone glowed with an eerie light.

"Mermista, is she controlling you somehow?" Adora asked. She turned to the queen. "Whatever you're doing, you stop that right now!"

Adora drew her sword. Bow notched an arrow into his bow. Glimmer teleported to Mermista, putting her body between her friend and the queen.

Queen Calypsa smiled calmly. She opened her mouth and began to sing. The song sounded beautiful and piercing at the same time.

"Sleep, sleep,

Surrender to the deep . . ."

Adora raised her sword over her head.

"For the honor of—" she began.

Then everything went black.

CHAPTER 3
CATRA'S PLAN

Catra paced back and forth across the metal floor of the force captains' barracks. Her pointed ears twitched, her long tail swung from side to side, and her eyes—one blue and one yellow—gleamed with anger.

"I can't believe I put you in charge once, just once, and you blew it!" she was saying. "I mean, I can understand Kyle, Rogelio, and Lonnie failing. But I had faith in you, Scorpia! And you failed!"

Scorpia, who towered above Catra, was an impressive soldier with a poisonous tail and two massive, powerful pincers instead of hands. But she looked frightened of her commander.

"I was ready to put my life on the line to defend that fortress, Catra," Scorpia said. "And I did. I took on She-Ra all by myself. But we were outnumbered."

Catra stopped and began counting on her sharp-clawed fingers. "It was you, Kyle, Rogelio, and Lonnie against Adora, Glimmer, Bow, Mermista, Frosta, and Perfuma. You weren't *that* outnumbered."

"Well, Kyle doesn't really count, does he?" Scorpia asked, mentioning the weakest member of the squad. "And Adora transforms into She-Ra, so she's technically two people. So that would bring the count to . . ."

"That's not the point!" Catra cried. "I trusted you! And I'm not sure if I can trust you again."

"You can absolutely trust me!" Scorpia promised. "There is nobody more loyal to you in the whole

Fright Zone than I am! We're besties! Buds! I'm the number two to your number one. I'm the night to your day. I'm the—"

"Okay, I get it!" Catra said impatiently. "You might not be perfect, but you're all I've got right now. So I guess I'm stuck with you."

Scorpia threw her arms around Catra and squeezed her. "There's nobody else I'd rather be stuck with, Catra!"

Catra scowled and wriggled out of her grasp. "I didn't ask you here for a hug fest. You're here because we're going on another mission."

Scorpia's eyes widened. "A mission? Me and you?"

"And a troop of soldiers," Catra replied. "Apparently, there's a new queen in Salineas, and she wants an audience with the Horde."

"And Hordak is sending us? That's awesome,"

Scorpia said. "What exactly does she want?"

"The queen isn't sure whether she will align with the Horde or with the princesses," Catra replied. "She wants to meet with us and decide."

"I don't know if you know this, but I have excellent negotiating skills," Scorpia said. "Just the other day I solved an argument between Kyle and Rogelio over who should get the bottom bunk."

"Oh yeah? How'd you do that?" Catra asked.

Scorpia clicked her pincers. "I cut the bunk bed in half so they both had the bottom," she answered. "Pretty clever, huh?"

"Well, we won't need negotiating skills for this," Catra said. "Because we're not going to negotiate."

Scorpia frowned. "We're not?"

Catra tapped a screen on the wall, and a blueprint of Salineas popped up.

"This new queen—Queen Calypsa—is leaving the Sea Gate open for us," Catra said, pointing. "That's why we're bringing soldiers with us. We'll sail in, take over Salineas, and get rid of the queen. It'll be as easy as taking field rations from Kyle."

Scorpia nodded. "That's smart thinking, Catra," she said. "Just one thing. If the queen asked for a meeting with the princesses, too, then won't She-Ra be there?"

Catra knew what Scorpia was getting at. Hordak had warned Catra to stop trying to go after Adora, and to concentrate on the missions he gave her. But this time, she could do both at once.

Catra smiled. "If Adora is there, that will be a bonus," she said. "First, we'll take Salineas for Lord Hordak. Then we'll make sure Adora and her friends don't stand in our way ever again."

Scorpia put an arm around Catra.

"And I'll be with you every step of the way!" she promised.

Catra frowned. Then she nodded to Scorpia. "Come on," she said. "We're going to Salineas!"

CHAPTER 4
CAPTURED!

"Adora? Adora, are you all right?"

Adora slowly opened her eyes to see Glimmer leaning over her, concern on her face. Her whole body felt weird, almost as if it was floating. Sitting up, she realized why. She, Glimmer, and Bow were in some type of bubble, floating in the air in a room with walls that looked like coral. Adora had the feeling they were no longer in Mermista's palace.

"Wh-what happened?" she asked, and then she instinctively reached for her sword. "And where is my sword?"

"You have been relieved of your sword, as your

friends have been relieved of their weapons."

Adora looked down. Queen Calypsa stood beneath the bubble, with Mermista close by.

"Sorry, guys, I tried to warn you," Mermista said.

I'm slipping, Adora scolded herself. *Once again, I've been blindsided. And I've lost my sword!*

Her confidence was shaken, but she knew that she shouldn't reveal that to the queen. She glared at Calypsa. "Your song. It did something to us. It put us to sleep."

"I think she's a sorceress," Glimmer said. Behind Calypsa, Mermista slowly nodded.

"A sorceress who has some kind of spell on Mermista," Adora guessed, and Mermista nodded again, without Calypsa seeing her.

Bow frowned. "Wait a second. I thought you asked us here because you wanted to talk about

joining forces with Etheria! Why are we in this magical bubble thing?"

Queen Calypsa laughed.

"Queen Angella is so trusting!" she said. "She sent
her own daughter into danger without a thought. I
have no intention of joining forces with Etheria. In
fact, I want to destroy the princesses!"

"Why? What did we ever do to you?" Glimmer
asked.

Calypsa's expression darkened. "Are you really so
ignorant in the crimes of your people, Princess?
You destroyed my kingdom, and now I will join
forces with Lord Hordak and destroy you. I invited
you here just so I could capture you. You will be an
excellent bargaining tool in my negotiations with
the Horde."

"The Horde doesn't like to negotiate," Adora told

her. "Let us out of here. You're going to need help defending Salineas when they get here."

"When I tell them I have the princess of Bright Moon and the great She-Ra as hostages, they will negotiate, not attack," the queen said confidently.

"We're underwater," Mermista burst out. "This place is like a maze. The only way out is—"

"Silence!" Queen Calypsa cried, and just like in the throne room, Mermista's hand flew to her mouth.

"*Mmmmmffff!*" Mermista complained.

"I will not stand by and let you help your friends," Queen Calypsa said. "Although there is no help for them as long as they are trapped inside my magical bubble. Now come!"

She turned and marched off. Mermista followed her, walking stiffly, as though her legs were moving on their own. Mermista caught Adora's eyes as she passed, and her gaze dropped to the stone floor below them.

She's trying to tell me something, Adora realized. *But what?*

"That Queen Calypsa might have some powerful magic," she said out loud. "But she's not very smart if she thinks she can make a deal with the Horde. They'll take over Salineas and come find us, and leave her with nothing."

"She's also delusional," Glimmer added. "I don't know what she's talking about, but the princesses have never destroyed anyone's kingdom!"

"We need to get out of here, find our weapons, and save Mermista before the Horde gets here," Bow said. He bounced up and down on the magic bubble. "This thing is strong!"

"It's magical," Glimmer reminded him. "But so are my sparkles. Stand back!"

Bow and Adora backed away from Glimmer. The princess closed her eyes and thrust out her arms. *Bam!* A burst of sparkles exploded from her fingertips. The bubble burst, and the three friends tumbled to the floor. Unhurt, they quickly got to their feet.

"You're right, Adora," Glimmer said. "That queen isn't smart. She had no idea my sparkles could get us out of that bubble."

Then she looked up. "I could try to teleport us out of here, but I'm not sure where we are—or where we'd end up."

"Mermista said that this place is a maze," Adora said. "And then she looked down at the floor. I think she was trying to tell me something."

They all looked down.

"Look!" Bow cried, pointing. "There's a sparkly thing down there."

Adora followed his gaze and picked up something flat, shiny, green, and no bigger than her fingernail.

"That looks like one of the scales on the queen's dress," Glimmer remarked.

"There's another one down there!" Bow added, pointing to the hallway that Mermista and the queen had just entered.

"I think it's some kind of trail," Adora guessed. "Let's follow it!"

She quickly took in her surroundings as they headed down the hallway. Mermista had said this place was underwater. It should have been dark, but the pink walls of coral glowed with a soft, magical light. They found a sparkling green scale about every ten feet, and followed the trail through a labyrinth of twisting, turning, narrow halls. In some spots, colorful fish and plants had been painted on the pink walls.

"It's actually really beautiful in here," Glimmer remarked as they walked. "But I'm starting to feel like we're never going to get out!"

Adora, leading the group, looked for another scale but didn't see one. She continued down the hall—nothing. Then the hall forked into two directions.

"The trail has ended," she announced. "We're on our own."

"We can't be far from the exit," Bow guessed. "Let's try this way first."

He jogged down the right branch of the fork,

and Adora and Glimmer followed. They made a right turn, and the tunnel opened up into a room. They entered and saw that the room was empty— and had ten open doors leading to ten more tunnels.

"Really?!" Adora said. "We don't have time to play 'guess the tunnel.' We need a strategy."

Glimmer frowned. "Like what?"

"I'm not sure," Adora said. "But there must be some logical way to do this. Like, we should make our own trail, and when we come to a dead end, we can follow it back to where we last started."

"Or we could just follow that sound," Bow said.

"What sound?" Adora asked, but as she spoke the words, she heard singing.

"Oh no! Is Calypsa back?" Glimmer asked.

They cautiously moved forward, and the singing

became louder. Adora grinned. She knew that voice well.

"I'm stuck in a bubble, it's true, it's true!

Do you like bubbles? I once did, too!

I used to ride on the waves through the deepest blue,

But now I'm stuck here without you . . ."

"Sea Hawk!" Adora cried.

CHAPTER 5
THE STORY OF THE SEA SORCERESS

Adora, Glimmer, and Bow raced toward the sound of their friend's voice. They turned left, and then right, and then left . . . and then they came to a giant magic bubble with a man inside who looked every inch a sea captain with his jaunty mustache, red bandanna, and gold-trimmed blue jacket.

"Blustering barnacles! Is this a vision I see? A hallucination brought on by days of loneliness in this magical prison?" Sea Hawk asked.

"No, it's really us!" Bow said.

"We were trying to escape from here when we heard your voice," Glimmer explained.

"Escape? Were you not trapped in a bubble, too? How, then, did you escape?" Sea Hawk asked.

Glimmer's purple eyes twinkled. "It just takes a second. Hang on."

She pointed at the bubble. *Bam!* It exploded in a shower of sparkles, and Sea Hawk tumbled to the floor. He jumped up, put his hand on his hip, and struck a jaunty pose.

"Thank you, Sprinkles! Your marvelous sparkles have prevailed, and now I can partake in the sweet taste of freedom!" he cried, pumping his fist in the air. Then he deflated. "Mermista! We must save her! I fear she has suffered a horrible fate."

"She's alive," Adora informed him. "But that Queen Calypsa is controlling her somehow."

Sea Hawk nodded. "Yes, through the amulet."

"I knew it!" Glimmer said. "It has something to do with that green stone around Mermista's neck, right?"

"The queen wears a green ring that allows her to control the amulet, and with the amulet, she controls Mermista's movements," Sea Hawk explained. "Mermista can talk if Calypsa lets her, but she cannot escape. And that's not all. If Calypsa says the right words, the amulet will turn Mermista into a puddle of water in an instant!"

Glimmer gasped. "That's horrible!"

"Wait, how did Calypsa get the amulet on Mermista in the first place?" Bow asked.

"I fear that I am to blame," Sea Hawk said. "But I will tell you my tale as we walk. The exit is not far, and I know the way."

Sea Hawk continued his story as they traveled

through the halls. "Several days ago, I was sailing the seas on my new ship, the finest ship to ever sail the seas. A strong wind blew my hair, and the sun shone overhead, smiling on my journey, for even the weather is my friend! Then I heard a song—a strange and beautiful song that compelled me to sail in its direction. I did, and then the song changed, and though I struggled with all my mighty might, I fell asleep."

"Calypsa put us to sleep, too!" Bow said.

Sea Hawk nodded. "When I awoke, I found myself trapped in a bubble. I did not know where I was," he went on. "Then that green, fiendish woman appeared, with my Mermista. She tricked Mermista and told her that I was in trouble. My dear, sweet Mermista came to save me! But Calypsa sang her song again, and she slipped the amulet onto

Mermista's neck. When we awoke, she explained the amulet's terrifying powers."

"And she left you down here, and brought Mermista back to the palace at Salineas," Glimmer deduced.

Sea Hawk nodded. "I have been so worried, wondering what has happened to her!" he said. "Now we must make this right turn, and we are almost there."

"How do you know the way out, if you woke up in the bubble?" Adora wondered.

"Calypsa and Mermista returned several times to give me rations," Sea Hawk explained. "I listened carefully to the pattern of their footsteps. We are almost there."

They walked past an open room, and Adora peered in. On the wall, there was a huge map of an underwater kingdom, and bubbles floating in the room held different objects: a mermaid doll, a necklace of sea stones, a jewel-studded goblet . . .

Adora stopped. "What's all this?"

"This must be what is left of Calypsa's old kingdom, the one that was destroyed," Sea Hawk guessed. "When I was in the bubble, she told me a harrowing tale of how the princesses attacked the kingdom of Corala with their armies of laser cannons."

"Princesses don't use laser cannons," Glimmer said.

Adora looked thoughtful. "Corala?" she repeated. "The battle of Corala was talked about in all our cadet history classes. It was one of Lord Hordak's great triumphs."

Glimmer studied the mural on the wall, which showed pod-shaped vehicles attacking a kingdom at the bottom of the sea.

"Those are symbols of Bright Moon on those pods!" she cried. "But it can't be!"

Adora studied the art. "You're right. It can't be," she said. "My guess is that Hordak used the symbols to trick the defenders of Corala into thinking that princesses were approaching. Then when they got close . . ."

". . . the Horde attacked!" Bow finished.

"And Queen Calypsa has blamed the princesses ever since," Adora said.

"That is correct," Sea Hawk told her. "The survivors of the attack sought refuge all over Etheria. Calypsa was just a young girl, and she ended up all alone, on an island. She was born with the ability to control magic, and she would have become a skilled sorceress had she been trained in Mystacor. But she was all alone, and she taught herself to manipulate magic without any teachers. For years, she planned her revenge on the princesses, and her powers got stronger and stronger. As soon as she came into her full powers, she began rebuilding Corala."

"It's a shame she didn't end up in Mystacor," Glimmer remarked. "She would have learned the truth there, and learned how to use her powers to do good."

"It's so sad," Bow added. "Everything—her whole life—is based on a lie."

"I understand what that's like," Adora said. "I thought all princesses were evil until I met you, remember?"

"Do not allow yourselves to feel sorry for her," Sea Hawk said. "She is a powerful sorceress. When she joins forces with the Horde, they will use her to destroy all of Etheria."

Adora frowned. "I hadn't thought of that," she said. "Maybe she's smart after all."

"Smart and dangerous," Bow pointed out.

"Come on, let's get out of here!" Adora urged.

Sea Hawk led them out of the room and into a dead end with a ladder going up the wall and a clear bubble overhead.

"I guess that's the way out," Glimmer said.

One by one, they climbed up the ladder and into the bubble, which was surrounded by the water of the ocean.

"That's right—Mermista said that this place was underwater," Adora said. "I wonder how deep we are?"

"I guess we'll find out soon," Glimmer said.

"What happens now?" Bow wondered. He tapped on the side of the bubble.

The bottom of the bubble closed up, and the whole bubble began to float up toward the surface of the ocean.

"Adventure!" Sea Hawk cheered.

Bow tapped the wall of the bubble again. "This one isn't magic. It's made out of some kind of clear, strong material."

"Where is this taking us, I wonder?" Adora asked.

"I have no idea," Sea Hawk admitted.

The bubble surfaced, bobbing in the sunlight above the water. It floated on top of the ocean, holding its four passengers. In the distance rose the Sea Gate and behind it, Salineas.

Glimmer frowned. "Too far to teleport," she said. "And we're far from Bright Moon, so I need to reserve my powers."

Bow gently pushed against the wall of the bubble, and it rolled forward. "If we all do it, we'll get there fast," he said.

They all pushed, and the ball zoomed toward

the Sea Gate. Suddenly, the water began to churn all around them.

"Maybe we're going too fast," Glimmer said.

"We couldn't be going *that* fast," Adora said. "But it might be—"

Rooooowwwwrrrrr!

With a mighty cry, a huge sea monster emerged from the waves!

CHAPTER 6
MONSTER TROUBLE

The monster had a snake-like body with sleek, black skin. Its head—if you could call it that—was a bulbous knob at the top of its body, with a circle of a mouth filled with snapping teeth. Wavy tentacles and blue and yellow gems surrounded its fierce jaws.

"Didn't you take care of this guy the last time we came to Salineas, Adora?" Glimmer asked.

"I thought so," Adora said. "But I guess it bounced back."

"That's right!" Sea Hawk said. "You stole my thunder by smiting this beast with your sword."

Roooowwwwwrrr!

"A sword that I don't have right now," Adora admitted, mentally kicking herself.

"And I don't have my arrows, either," Bow added.

The sea monster smacked its head against their transport bubble. It didn't break the bubble, but it sent them bouncing across the waves. The four friends lost their footing and bumped into one another as the bubble careened across the ocean. The sea monster dove into the water and swam after them.

I can't let my friends down again! Adora thought.

"We've got to find a way to defend ourselves," she said out loud.

"We seem to be safe inside the bubble," Glimmer said. "If we can get close to shore, I might be able to teleport us all out of here."

Bam! The sea monster head-butted them again.

"Aaaaaaaaaaaaaaaaah!"

Everyone screamed as the bubble flew up, up, up into the air.

Then it plummeted down, down, down to the waves.

Wham! It hit the water with strong force, and then bounced again.

"We're moving *away* from the shore," Adora pointed out.

"We can't stop the monster without weapons," Bow said.

Suddenly, Sea Hawk began to sing.

"Come to me, my friend of the sea,

Wicked and awesome and wild and free.

Come to me, my ocean friend,

Before I reach a tragic end!"

"Sea Hawk, this is no time for singing!" Glimmer scolded him.

The sea monster was gaining on them again. The water around their bubble began to whirl and churn. Before the sea monster could reach them, another creature arose from the depths, this one twice as big as the monster chasing them. It looked like a giant, purple octopus, with eight wiggling tentacles and large, yellow eyes in its enormous head.

Bow's eyes got wide. "Two monsters?"

Sea Hawk grinned. "Nellie, my old girl!" he called out. "I knew you wouldn't let me down. Can you take care of this fiend for us?"

Nellie gently placed a tentacle on top of the bubble. Then she faced the snakelike sea monster. A shrill, shrieking noise came from her beak-like mouth, and she wrapped the creature in her tentacles. It thrashed and roared, but she held on. Then the two of them disappeared beneath the waves.

"Thank you, fair Nellie!" Sea Hawk called out. "I shall not forget you!"

"Awesome!" Bow cheered.

"Is she a friend of yours?" Glimmer asked.

"I have met many friends in the sea on my travels," Sea Hawk answered. "Nellie and I go way back. She happens to like my singing."

"Let's get to shore before we meet any more monsters," Adora suggested, and they pushed the bubble across the waves once more.

Soon they reached the rocky coastline.

"There doesn't seem to be a door in this bubble," Bow said. "How are we supposed to get out?"

"Let me see if I have enough juice to get us to land," Glimmer said. She put her arms around all of them. "Group hug!"

They teleported onto the shore in a shower of

sparkles. Glimmer took a deep breath. "Four! That might be a personal record."

Adora scanned the surroundings. "There's no sign of the Horde," she said. "If we can talk to Queen Calypsa and explain what really happened to her kingdom, she'll close the gate and we can save Salineas."

"*And* get her to release Mermista," Bow added.

"I fear that your plan is destined to fail," Sea Hawk said. "You will not be able to talk, because Calypsa will sing her dangerous song as soon as she sees you."

"We have to try," Adora said. "First, we'll get our weapons back. Then Glimmer can teleport and catch the queen by surprise."

"I think I have at least one more teleport in me," Glimmer said with a grin.

"Great!" Adora said. "And when you teleport to the queen, you can put a hand over her mouth right away, so she can't sing."

Sea Hawk shook his head. "It is too dangerous," he said. "She will use her magic against Glimmer. There is no way to stop her song."

Glimmer turned to Sea Hawk and grinned. "Maybe we can't stop it," she said. "But I have another idea . . ."

CHAPTER 7
THE SOUND OF VICTORY

"The weapons hold is behind the throne room," Sea Hawk whispered as he crept around the back of the palace with Adora, Bow, and Glimmer. "We should be able to enter through the window."

He stopped and pointed upward. Adora jumped and grabbed on to the edge of the open window, then pulled herself up so that she could peer inside. Two Salinean guards flanked the door on the opposite wall, their backs to the window. She spotted her sword hanging on the wall behind them, as well as Bow's bow and quiver full of arrows.

Adora dropped back down. "This looks pretty easy," she said. "Glimmer, I know that last teleport took a lot out of you. Can you pop in there, get our weapons, and get back out?"

Glimmer grinned. "Should be a snap," she answered. "I'll be in and out in a flash!" She disappeared in a cloud of purple glitter.

Whoot! Whoot! Whoot! An alarm sounded.

Glimmer appeared back in front of them, her arms filled with the sword, bow, and quiver. "Well, that didn't go as smoothly as I thought."

"We need to get out of here!" Sea Hawk warned.

Adora and Bow took their weapons. Before they could run, the two guards jumped out of the window.

"I've got this!" Bow said. He quickly notched one

of his trick arrows and let it fly. A net attached to the arrow opened up and trapped the two guards.

"Hurry!" Glimmer yelled.

They raced to the castle entrance. The two guards there crossed their long tridents, blocking the way.

"We demand to see Queen Calypsa!" Adora said.

"We have orders to let no one in except for the Horde," one of the guards replied.

"Are you sure you don't want to just step aside?" Adora asked. "That would be the easy way."

"We cannot let you pass!" said the other.

"Fine," Adora said. "I guess we'll do this the hard way, then."

She grinned and looked at her sword. Then she raised it above her head. "For the honor of Grayskull!"

The sword grew brighter and brighter. Adora floated up into the air, bathed in light. Her body spun, and her hair fell loose from its ponytail.

When the light faded, She-Ra stood there, a vision in white and gold with a red cape that flowed behind her. The two guards stared at her, open-mouthed.

"I don't think Mermista would want me to hurt you," she said. "But right now, I need to get you out of the way."

She picked up one guard in each hand. Then she tossed one to the left and one to the right. Both guards went flying.

She-Ra nodded to her friends. "Ready?"

"Ready!" they replied.

They marched into the throne room.

"What took you so long?" Mermista asked. Adora had been friends with Mermista long enough to know that she used her sarcasm to protect her true feelings. Mermista was happy to see them.

Queen Calypsa stood up.

"You've escaped!" she cried. "But how foolish you are. Your weapons are no match for my song."

She opened her mouth, but before any sound came out, Sea Hawk took a big conch shell from his belt, raised it to his lips, and began to sing through it.

"My name is Sea Hawk—yes, that's me!

I'm the finest captain you'll ever see!

I ride on the waves through the deepest blue,

With the excellent help of my expert crew.

And if you're in trouble,

You can call on me.

I'll come to your rescue,

And set you free!"

Sea Hawk's loud, boisterous singing, amplified by

the shell, completely drowned out Calypsa's song.
She glared at him.

"What is that horrible music?" she asked. "Stop
that immediately!"

"They call me Sea Hawk—yes, they do!

I sing when I sail the ocean blue.

I sing the songs of the mighty sea.

I'll sing and I'll sing and you can't stop me . . ."

Queen Calypsa grimaced and put her hands over
her ears. Adora and her team sprang into action.

Zing! Bow trapped Queen Calypsa in one of his
net arrows.

Poof! Glimmer teleported to Mermista and
pulled the amulet off her neck.

"Finally!" Mermista cried, and she lunged at
Queen Calypsa, tackling her and pinning her to the
floor. She pulled the green ring off the queen's
finger and slipped it onto her own.

"Glimmer, put that necklace on Calypsa, now!" Mermista cried.

Glimmer did as Mermista asked, and Mermista released her grip on the queen.

"Foolish girl," Calypsa said. "Your pirate can't sing forever. I will sing again, and when I do—"

"Silence!" Mermista yelled, pointing the finger wearing the ring at the queen.

The queen's hand flew to her mouth. Her green eyes glared at Mermista, who controlled the amulet now.

She grinned. "How does this ring work again?" she asked. "I can turn you into a puddle of water, right?"

A look of horror dawned on Calypsa's face as she realized how helpless she was. Her fate was now in the hands of the princess she had held captive.

"Yeah, that sounds like it might be fun," Mermista said, and she pointed the ring at the queen.

CHAPTER 8
WHAT DID WE FORGET . . . ?

"Mermista, no!" She-Ra yelled.

Mermista dropped her finger and turned to her friend. "You are no fun," she said.

"I know Calypsa has done some pretty bad things," She-Ra said. "But she was tricked by the Horde. She saw her whole kingdom destroyed when she was just a kid."

"Uuugggh," Mermista groaned. "I know all about that. I guess you have a point. But can't I . . . I don't know, make her quack like a duck? Or dance? Or clean the bathrooms or something?"

"Just make sure she doesn't sing," She-Ra said. She turned to Sea Hawk. "I think you can stop now."

"*I am, I am!*" Sea Hawk finished. He took a deep breath. "Are you sure? I've got twelve more verses."

"No, we're good," She-Ra said. She glanced down at the queen, still tangled in Bow's net and unable to speak. "We just need to figure out what to do with Calypsa."

"I could order her to take a swim with some jellyfish," Mermista offered.

"I think we should bring her to Mystacor," Glimmer said. "Aunt Castaspella will know what to do with her."

"Just as long as you get her far away from here," Mermista said. "I can't believe I let her put that amulet on me. I feel like a total failure. I don't deserve to be in the Rebellion."

"Of course you do!" She-Ra said. "We're a team, and you're a part of it! We all have bad days, Mermista. You're being too hard on yourself."

Glimmer smirked. "You're right," she said. "Just like *you* were being too hard on yourself earlier."

"That was different," She-Ra said.

"Is it?" Glimmer asked. "Not everybody can succeed every time. Not even She-Ra. And that's okay."

"Um, aren't we all forgetting something?" Bow asked.

Glimmer frowned. "Like what?"

Bow shrugged. "I'm not sure, but I've got this nagging feeling—"

Boom! A loud explosion rocked the palace. Pieces of coral crumbled and showered down.

She-Ra spun around. "The Horde!"

CHAPTER 9
HEY, ADORA!

"Mermista, keep the queen quiet," She-Ra ordered. She raced out of the throne room. Bow, Sea Hawk, and Glimmer followed closely behind.

A line of Horde soldiers marched to the palace behind a Horde robot. The globe-shaped machine crawled up the steps on its metal, spiderlike legs. Its lone crystal eye glowed, gearing up for another blast.

"Not today!" She-Ra yelled, and she jumped onto the robot in one leap, thrusting her sword into the top of the globe. The bot sparked, sizzled, and stopped.

Meanwhile, the Horde soldiers charged forward, blasters ready.

Ziiiiiip! Bow fired a stun arrow at one of the soldiers, freezing him in his tracks.

Glimmer pointed at one of the soldiers' blasters, but only a few weak sparks shot from her fingertips.

"Uh-oh," Glimmer said. "I'm out of power."

"Never fear, Shimmer!" Sea Hawk jumped in front of her and tackled the soldier to the ground, wrestling the blaster from the soldier's hands.

She-Ra leapt off the fried robot to help her friends. Three more robots appeared behind the line of soldiers. She jumped on one of them just as it erupted in a blast aimed at Sea Hawk. He somersaulted out of the way just in time.

"Adventure!" he yelled.

"Hiiiyaaaah!" She-Ra thrust her sword into the

robot, and a shower of sparks shot up. She jumped to the next one and dispatched it with another blow from her sword. Just one more to go . . .

"Adora, look out!" Glimmer called.

She-Ra whipped her head around to see Catra and Scorpia advancing on the palace, riding in a robot three times as big as any regular Horde bot. It was walking on two metal legs as tall as trees. On the face of the bot was a huge wheel that spun around, shooting red laser blasts in all directions. One of the blasts zoomed toward She-Ra.

She jumped off the robot and out of the way just in time, ducking behind a wall of purple coral. *BOOM!* The laser blast hit the robot, exploding it into a pile of flaming wreckage.

"Hey, Adora!" Catra called. "Come out, come out, wherever you are!"

"Shouldn't you call her She-Ra when she's in her

princess form?" Scorpia asked. "I mean, it's kind of confusing, right?"

"She'll always be Adora to me," Catra replied.

She-Ra's mind raced. If she stayed where she was, Catra would blast the coral. If she ran, Catra would blast her. She could charge the robot and try to take it down from the legs, but it was a risk . . . a risk she had to try.

She launched into a run.

"There you are, Adora!" Catra said, and the laser cannons began to spin . . .

Whoooosh! A wave of water surged out of the castle, knocking down Horde soldiers in its path and slamming into the robot's legs. The base of the bot crashed to the ground, and water splashed up all around it.

"Sorry, the Horde isn't welcome in Salineas,"

Mermista said, and slammed the huge robot with another water blast.

The water receded, revealing the battered robot base with Catra and Scorpia still inside—and the cannon wheel still glowing and spinning. Catra grinned as a barrage of laser blasts exploded from the bot.

Mermista dodged out of the way, and She-Ra jumped on top of the bot. She pried open the cockpit and tossed out Scorpia, who tumbled to the ground. Mermista pointed to her feet, and a geyser sprung up underneath Scorpia, lifting her high into the air.

"Hey! Get me down from here!" Scorpia wailed.

She-Ra pointed her sword at Catra.

"Enough, Catra!" she demanded.

Catra jumped to her feet. "It won't be enough

until all of Etheria belongs to the Horde. Salineas will be ours!"

She lunged at She-Ra, pushing her and sending them both falling to the ground. Catra swiped at She-Ra with her sharp claws, and She-Ra rolled out of the way. Then she felt a jolt as Catra's stun-baton jabbed her in the leg. An attack like that might have flattened Adora, but She-Ra shook it off. She jumped to her feet and raised her sword over her head.

For a split second, she hesitated. She didn't want to fight Catra. Even after everything that had happened, she still held out hope that her friend would see the light. That hope had once been a burning flame, and now it was just a tiny spark. But it was still there.

Don't hold back, she told herself. *Catra is your enemy. She wants to destroy you.*

"Aaaaaaaaah!" With a mighty cry, she brought the sword down. Catra leapt out of the way with feline agility. Suddenly, she was behind She-Ra, kicking the backs of her knees. She-Ra buckled, but she didn't fall. She spun around and delivered a round kick to Catra's ankles, bringing her to her knees.

She-Ra pointed the sword at Catra's chest.

"Retreat, Catra!" she said. "Get out of here, and don't come back!"

Catra's eyes gleamed, and she grinned. "You're talking like someone who has the upper hand, Adora. But you don't. Look around."

Keeping her sword on Catra, She-Ra gazed around. Bow was surrounded by a circle of Horde soldiers. Scorpia had jumped off the geyser and had Sea Hawk in her claws. Mermista and Glimmer were nowhere in sight. Fear tightened She-Ra's throat. What had happened to her friends?

"This time, you're outnumbered!" Catra said, and behind her, a new wave of Horde soldiers marched up from the shore.

"Drop the sword, Adora," Catra continued. "You've lost!"

CHAPTER 10
TRUST

"Don't do it, Adora!"

Mermista ran down the walkway, followed by Calypsa, who had a hand over her mouth. Behind her, Glimmer pointed a trident at the sorceress's back.

"Mermista, what are you doing?" She-Ra asked.

"Just trust me and cover your ears," she said. Then she pointed to Calypsa, the green ring glittering on her finger. "Hit it."

Calypsa began to sing. Bow, Sea Hawk, Mermista, Glimmer, and She-Ra covered their ears. Catra frowned in confusion, but her eyes widened as the powerful song floated across the island.

"March, march, march away.

Back to your ship—

You will obey . . ."

Catra stood and straightened up. Scorpia dropped Sea Hawk. Then Catra, Scorpia, and every member of the Horde turned and marched back to their ship, leaving their battered robots behind.

She-Ra lowered her hands, and she, Sea Hawk, and Bow joined Mermista, Glimmer, and Calypsa at the castle entrance.

"Nice plan," She-Ra said.

"Thanks," Mermista said. "Once Glimmer ran out of sparkles, I had her keep an eye on Calypsa while I joined the battle. Once I saw how outnumbered we were, I figured I could use the power of the amulet to make Calypsa sing away the Horde for us."

"Awesome!" Bow said.

"It was certainly not awesome," Calypsa replied. "I would never willingly assist the princesses! Not after what they did to my people!"

She-Ra faced the sorceress. "Calypsa, we need to talk," she said. She transformed into Adora. "I think we have something in common."

"Um, while you guys have your heart-to-heart, I need to go close the Sea Gate," Mermista said. "That song's gonna wear off soon, and I want to make sure the Horde doesn't come back."

Mermista left, and Calypsa turned her back on Adora.

"I have nothing to say to you," Calypsa said coldly.

"You don't have to say anything," Adora said. "Just listen. I wasn't always a princess. I grew up in the Horde, where I was taught that princesses were evil. That princesses were trying to destroy Etheria."

"You were taught the truth," Calypsa said.

"No, that was a lie," Adora said. "I only learned that when I met Glimmer and Bow. The Horde is the real evil. They have been attacking innocent villages all around Etheria for years. And they attacked Corala."

Calypsa frowned. "That can't be. I was just a little girl, but I remember the flag of Bright Moon flying on the attacking robots."

Adora motioned to the sparking robots behind her. "Robots like these. Horde robots. The Horde used the symbol of Bright Moon to get close to your kingdom, and then attacked. When *I* was a little girl, we learned that the Horde had taken Corala in a great battle. We just weren't told how."

Confusion filled Calypsa's eyes. "But . . . everything I have known . . ."

"Is a lie," Adora finished for her. "That happened to me, too. But I couldn't ignore the truth once I opened my eyes. We have no reason to lie to you, Calypsa."

"How can I trust you?" Calypsa asked. "I do not know you."

"I didn't know Glimmer or Bow, either, when I first met them, but I could see the good in them," Adora said. "I was their enemy, and they protected me. When I decided to trust them, I became a better person."

She reached over and removed the amulet from around Calypsa's neck. "You may not trust me, yet, but I'll trust you."

Calypsa's eyes widened.

"Adora, are you sure?" Glimmer asked.

"No," Adora said, and she smiled at Calypsa. "But

I think Calypsa can go to Mystacor to live with other sorcerers, just like you suggested, Glimmer. What do you think, Calypsa?"

She didn't answer right away. "I think that I would like to go to Mystacor. I have so many questions, and it sounds like I might be able to find some answers there."

"Great!" Glimmer said. "Aunt Castaspella can keep an eye on you there."

"Mystacor is a long way off," Bow remarked.

Mermista returned. "Who's going to Mystacor?" she asked. Then she raised her eyebrows. "And why isn't Calypsa wearing the amulet?"

Adora quickly explained the plan.

"I was kind of hoping she would be locked up in prison for the rest of her life," Mermista said. "But if you want to be all compassionate or whatever, go ahead. Sea Hawk can bring her to Mystacor."

"Will you really send me away so soon, m'lady?" Sea Hawk asked.

"Something tells me you'll be back," Mermista replied.

Sea Hawk sighed. "Fine," he said, and then he brightened and put an arm around Calypsa. "Let us embark on our journey, then! I have so many shanties I can teach you. We can duet!"

"We don't have to do that," Calypsa said. "Quiet can be nice sometimes."

"Nonsense!" Sea Hawk cried. "Here, we'll start with one of my favorites.

"There once was a baby shrimp in the sea,

Who sang doo doo doo and dee dee dee . . ."

Calypsa cast a pleading look at the others as Sea Hawk swept her away. Mermista grinned.

"That's *almost* as good as prison for her, I guess," she said.

Adora handed her the amulet. "Here, you should have this."

Mermista took it, pulled the ring off her finger—and then promptly threw them both into the ocean. "*Nobody* should have those," she said. "I haven't thanked you guys yet. That whole situation was . . . bad."

"Don't worry about it," Adora said. "We've all been vulnerable before. But now we have each other."

"Now you're just getting mushy," Mermista said. "Why don't you take one of my boats and get out of here?"

Adora grinned. "I love you, too, Mermista," she said. She turned to Glimmer and Bow. "Let's get home."

Everyone said their goodbyes, and Adora, Bow, and Glimmer made their way to the Salineas docks.

"Are you feeling okay, Glimmer?" Adora asked.

"I'll be fine," Glimmer promised. "I've been through worse."

Bow looked at Adora. "You know what you said back there? About becoming a better person? Well, I feel that way, too."

"Me too," Glimmer added. "I don't know where we'd be now if we hadn't met in the woods that day."

"But we did!" Adora said. "And now we're the Best Friend Squad!"

"Three cheers for the Best Friend Squad!" Bow cried.

"All right, now this is getting a little silly," Glimmer said.

"Come on, you love it," Adora teased as the Salineas docks came into sight. The blue sea sparkled, stretching out into the horizon.

There might be more monsters out there, she thought. *Or more Horde ships.*

She looked at her friends. *But whatever happens, we'll be okay.*

ABOUT THE AUTHOR

Tracey West has written more than 300 books for children and young adults, including the following series: Pixie Tricks, Hiro's Quest, and Dragon Masters. She has appeared on the *New York Times* bestseller list as the author of the Pokémon chapter book adaptations. Tracey currently lives with her family in New York State's Catskill Mountains. She can be found on Twitter at @TraceyWestBooks.

Don't miss any of She-Ra's adventures!

She doesn't need a hero. She *is* a hero.

On a planet called Etheria, two forces battle for control. The Horde, with its skillfully trained soldiers and advanced technology, has one goal: to conquer all of Etheria in the name of Hordak. The other force, the Rebellion, is made up of princesses and has been fighting to maintain harmony and freedom for all of Etheria's people.

Hidden among them all is a hero to be. Her destiny was written by the First Ones a thousand years ago. Now she is about to rise again.

Her mission is to protect Etheria. But she can't do it alone.

After the battle of Bright Moon, the Horde army has retreated. But Adora knows they'll soon be back. Now the Princess Council is searching for a way to make the Rebellion stronger.

Then they discover a First Ones mural that shows an island full of animals with magical powers. Are these magical creatures real—and will they help the Rebellion?

Adora and her friends set out on a quest to investigate. But they aren't the only ones on Etheria looking to strengthen their cause . . .

CHECK OUT ADORA'S
REBEL PRINCESS GUIDE!

Underneath She-Ra, I'm still Adora, and I'm still getting used to life outside the Fright Zone. (Like, what's a birthday party?!) So I've been taking notes on everything.

Read on for a preview!

✦ SO, THIS IS WHAT HAPPENS
WHEN I TRANSFORM

IT'S HARD TO DESCRIBE WHAT IT FEELS LIKE when I transform into She-Ra. It's kind of like, "Whoa!" and then "What?" and then everything gets super bright. And then the light fades, and I feel bigger, stronger, and taller.

When I'm She-Ra, I feel like I can do anything. Like I'm unstoppable. My new outfit is pretty cool, too.

When I'm Adora, I pull back my hair to keep it out of my face while I'm in action. But when I'm She-Ra, having a mane of long, flowing hair just feels so right.

ME FINDING THE
SWORD

The Sword of
Protection is what
lets me transform
into She-Ra.

Are these the
coolest boots, or
what? Not only do
they look awesome, but
they're really comfortable.
I've tested them on ice, snow,
and mud, and I can run faster,
jump higher, and kick harder with
them on.

SO COOL!

THE SWORD OF PROTECTION

MY SWORD IS REALLY POWERFUL—which is why I don't understand why it didn't come with any instructions. I really can't wait to uncover all of its secrets.

STUFF I KNOW ABOUT MY SWORD

- It was made by the First Ones.

- I found it in the Whispering Woods.

- Nobody can use it to turn into She-Ra except for me. (At least, nobody I've met yet.)

- The runestone in the hilt is keyed to She-Ra, Princess of Power. You can see it sparkling in the hilt, but the blade of the sword is actually part of the runestone, too.

STUFF I DON'T KNOW ABOUT MY SWORD

- I know that my sword can change shapes, but I don't know how to control it yet! And why does it turn into useless stuff, like a mug, a jug, and a weird musical instrument?

- Light Hope says that one of the functions of the runestone is to "heal and restore balance." But no matter how hard I try, I can't figure out how to use the sword to heal anything!

GLIMMER

BACK IN THE FRIGHT ZONE, if you told me I'd become friends with a princess, I would have wrestled you. But Glimmer is a brave fighter and a great leader, and I'm proud to call her my friend.

THE MOONSTONE

KINGDOM: Bright Moon

RUNESTONE: The Moonstone

WEAPONS AND ACCESSORIES: She carries the magical staff that her dad, Micah, used to use in battle.

POWERS: Glimmer's main power is teleporting. And it's amazing when she hurls energy blasts and sparkle bombs at her attackers. Her powers are connected to the Moonstone.

FAMILY: Her mom is Queen Angella of Bright Moon. Her dad, King Micah, was a powerful sorcerer from Mystacor who died fighting the Horde. Her aunt Castaspella is a sorceress who lives in Mystacor.

LIKES: Leading the Rebellion; sneaking out of her room so she can hang out with me and Bow

DISLIKES: Cleaning her room; when she's far from Bright Moon and she runs out of power, because she's too far from the Moonstone

FAVORITE QUOTE: "No princess left behind!"

GLIMMER'S ROOM

WHEN I FIRST MET GLIMMER, I thought her room in the castle would be filled with frilly princess stuff. And while it is kind of frilly, it's the perfect quarters for the leader of the Rebellion.

Glimmer's bed reminds me of a bird's nest in a tree. She can teleport up to her bed, but if her friends want to hang with her there, we need to climb up these steps.

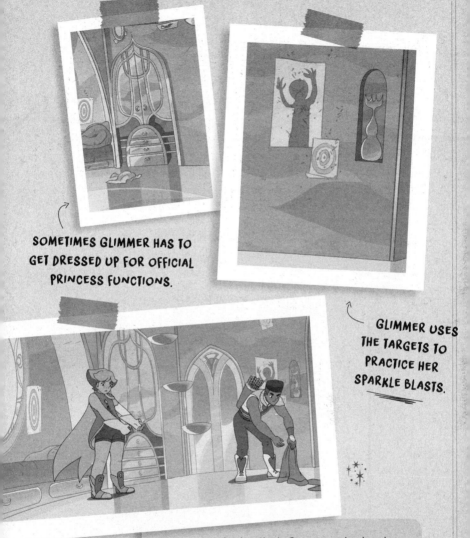

SOMETIMES GLIMMER HAS TO GET DRESSED UP FOR OFFICIAL PRINCESS FUNCTIONS.

GLIMMER USES THE TARGETS TO PRACTICE HER SPARKLE BLASTS.

I LOVE MY FRIENDS!

Glimmer's lucky that Bow can't stand messes, because he usually cleans up after her.

BOW

BOW WAS NICE TO ME right from the start, even though he thought I was his enemy. That's just the kind of person he is.

KINGDOM: Bright Moon

WEAPONS AND ACCESSORIES: Bow designs trick arrows that he
shoots from a collapsible bow. He's a great inventor. He built a
tracker pad that can detect magic, First Ones tech, and
Horde signals.

POWERS: Bow doesn't have any magic powers, like a princess or a
sorcerer would. But I don't think he needs them. He's really
skilled with any weapon you put in his hands.

FAMILY: Bow's dads take care of the library in the Whispering
Woods. They are fascinated with First Ones tech, which is
probably why Bow is so good at figuring it out. He has
twelve older siblings who are all historians.

LIKES: Technology; fighting with the Rebellion; hanging out
with Glimmer
♡

DISLIKES: The Horde; arguing with Glimmer

FAVORITE QUOTE: "Best Friend Squad to the rescue!"

HE CAN GO HEAD-TO-HEAD
IN COMBAT WITH A HORDE
SOLDIER ANY DAY!

BOW'S ♡
TRICK ARROWS

BOW'S TRICK ARROWS ARE very impressive. He always seems to have the right arrow for just the right situation. Here are a few of them:

LASSO ARROW: A rope uncoils in midair and wraps around whatever Bow is aiming at.

NET ARROW: When Bow shoots the arrow, a chamber opens up and releases a net that surrounds his opponent.

WOW!!

SLIME ARROW: I'm still not exactly sure what this one is for, but it's awesomely gross.

STUN ARROW: Can freeze an enemy in its tracks.

FLARE ARROW: Lights up.

SONIC ARROW: This arrow makes a loud, booming noise when it lands.

BOW'S
TRACKER PAD

Bow's invention helps us track down First Ones tech and find our bearings when we're lost. It can also warn us when the Horde is nearby. Bow is always making improvements to it.

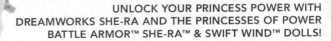

A NETFLIX ORIGINAL SERIES

DREAMWORKS

SHE-RA
AND THE
PRINCESSES OF POWER

NOW STREAMING | NETFLIX

UNLOCK YOUR PRINCESS POWER WITH
DREAMWORKS SHE-RA AND THE PRINCESSES OF POWER
BATTLE ARMOR™ SHE-RA™ & SWIFT WIND™ DOLLS!

Colors and decorations may vary. Ages 6+.